The Boxcar Children Mysteries

THE MYSTERY CRUISE

created by
GERTRUDE CHANDLER WARNER

Illustrated by Charles Tang

ALBERT WHITMAN & Company
Morton Grove, Illinois

ISBN 0-8075-5368-9

3 5 7 9 10 8 6 4

Printed in the U.S.A.

Contents

CHAPTER 1

The West Wind

On the plane, Benny Alden, for the tenth time, looked through the brochure filled with pictures of the *West Wind*. They were *really* on their way to the cruise ship waiting for them in Miami. All the Aldens were going to sail to the Caribbean Sea.

Benny tugged at his sister's sleeve, pointing to a picture of a pool. "Look at this, Jessie. We can go swimming every day." He flipped over the page. "And we can play volleyball, too."

1

Jessie smiled. "Yes, and we can play badminton and basketball and all kinds of games, Benny. You'll see."

Yawning, she stretched. They had awakened very early to travel from Greenfield, Massachusetts, to Boston. There they had caught a plane going to Miami, Florida.

At last they were ready to land. Jessie was sure her heart was beating just as fast as Benny's. But he had an excuse. He was only six. Being twelve, Jessie thought she should act more grown up. But today she didn't care. She felt like jumping up and down.

She glanced at her sister and brother across the aisle, but ten-year-old Violet and fourteen-year-old Henry had their eyes glued to the window. She knew they were excited, too.

The pilot's voice came over the intercom, interrupting her thoughts. "Ladies and gentlemen, we'll be landing at the Miami airport in fifteen minutes. Please fasten your seat belts."

Fascinated, Benny stared down at the tall white buildings lining the coast and the ships dotting the harbor. "I wonder which ship is ours," he said.

Grandfather, sitting in front of Benny, turned around. "The *West Wind* will be waiting for us at the wharf, Benny."

Benny bounced up and down. "I wish we were on board right now! This is going to be the best trip you've ever taken us on, Grandfather."

"I think so, too," Violet added.

James Alden chuckled. His grandchildren always appreciated whatever he did for them. It was a pleasure to take them places. And a cruise would be a most enjoyable vacation for him, too.

Contentedly, Mr. Alden leaned back in his seat. How fortunate he was to have found his four grandchildren. To think they'd once hidden from him in an old boxcar, believing he was a mean old man. When they came to live with him, though, it wasn't long before they loved and trusted him.

The plane dropped, and Benny squeezed his eyes shut, anticipating the cruise. Would there be a mystery on board the ship? It seemed that wherever they went something mysterious happened.

When the plane had landed and taxied to a stop, the Aldens walked down the steps. In the distance a small bus with the words "American Cruise Lines" on it was waiting for them.

After boarding the bus, Violet sat next to Jessie. Suddenly her hand flew to her cheek. "Oh, I think I forgot to pack my sneakers."

Jessie shook her head. "No, Violet. I saw you put them in your bag."

Violet sighed with relief. "Good. I know I packed my best dress, shorts, pants, two bathing suits, and four tops."

"That's plenty," Jessie replied. "There's a laundry room on board, so we can do at least one washing."

The bus rumbled down to the docks and stopped with a jerk. "Here we are, folks," the driver said, opening the door. "All out for a cruise of a lifetime."

Benny leaped up and hurried down the aisle. "Thanks for the ride, mister."

Once outside, he stopped dead still, his mouth dropping open. "The *West Wind* is beautiful!" He bent his head back to look up at the huge ship, his eyes scanning the gleaming white hull from stem to stern. A red smokestack loomed above the three main decks, and toward the bow the American flag fluttered smartly in the breeze. People on board leaned over the railing and waved. Enthusiastically, Benny waved back.

Henry stood beside Benny, his hand resting lightly on his brother's shoulder. "Isn't it something, Benny? We're going to have a great time!"

"You said it!" Benny answered.

A man in a white uniform smiled at them and motioned them to come aboard.

Grandfather went first, followed by Jessie, Henry, Benny, and Violet.

"Do you have a table reserved for dinner?" the man asked.

"Yes, our travel agent arranged for a table for six. I suppose one more guest will be seated with us," Grandfather said, "in order to fill the table."

"I see," the man said. "Then the steward will show you to your cabins."

Another young man in a uniform greeted them. "Follow me," he said politely. "A fire drill is scheduled at eleven. Please don't forget."

He led them to their cabins. Violet and Jessie were pleased at their large cabin with twin beds, a dressing table, and a small bathroom. Henry and Benny's cabin had bunk beds while Grandfather had a single cabin only a few doors away.

Benny ran to the ladder and climbed to the top bed. "Can I have the top bunk, Henry?" he asked, plumping up the pillow.

"That's fine by me," Henry answered, opening the closet and hanging up his new navy blazer.

After unpacking, the children met outside on the deck. Their cabins were on B deck.

Benny looked about at the deck chairs, the shiny floors, and the portholes of the staterooms. "Wow! It's so big," he said. "I wish

I'd brought my roller skates."

Henry laughed. "And what if a wind tilted the ship? You'd go sliding right off the deck into the ocean."

"Not me!" Benny protested. "I'm a good skater. I'd be able to stay on my feet."

"Come on," Henry urged. "Let's look around. The ship sails at ten o'clock and it's nine o'clock now."

"We have an hour to explore the ship," Jessie said, walking over to the stairs.

They went up to A deck and were amazed at how many shops there were.

"Need a haircut, Benny?" Henry asked, pointing to a barber shop.

"No way. I don't want to waste a minute." Benny touched his hair. "I look fine," he pronounced.

They laughed, going past a beauty shop, a jewelry store, a drug store, a perfume shop, and a theater. They went down to C Deck where a gym was located. A nearby room contained the latest exercise equipment.

Back to B Deck, close to their rooms, they explored the laundry room, the game room, and the library. They didn't have time to go up to the sun deck to see the swimming pool, for a large blast from the ship's horn warned them that it was almost sailing time.

They hurried to meet Grandfather at the railing. Passengers were waving and shouting to friends below.

Red, white, and blue streamers and confetti floated in the air. A Dixieland band, playing a lively tune, was on the deck in back of them. There was a mighty horn blast and the ship moved slowly away from the wharf.

Benny danced a few steps in time to the music, then came back to the railing to wave and yell, "Good-bye, everybody!"

The white buildings on shore slowly receded into the distance.

Jessie squeezed Violet's hand. "Isn't this beautiful?"

"Yes, oh, yes," Violet answered.

The Aldens stood on the deck until Miami was only a dot.

Grandfather tapped Benny on the shoulder. "How about a glass of milk and a pastry?"

Benny nodded, always ready to eat. He went over to a long table with doughnuts, sweet rolls, fresh fruit, and beverages. He helped himself to a chocolate doughnut and milk. Jessie, Violet, and Henry had a snack, too, even though they'd had a small breakfast on the plane. But that seemed like days ago instead of just hours.

"I found out who will be at the table in the dining room with us," Grandfather said, sipping a cup of steaming coffee.

"Who?" Jessie asked, giving a waiter her empty plate and glass. "I hope he's nice."

"Where is he?" Benny asked, finishing his milk.

"He's over there," Grandfather said, with a nod of his head. "I've already talked to him. His name is Max Greene and he seems like a nice fellow. Would you like to meet him?"

"Could we?" Violet asked.

Henry looked at the man leaning over the

rail. He had a black beard and wore a cap to shade his eyes.

"Max," Grandfather said, moving to his side. "I'd like you to meet my grandchildren — Violet, Benny, Henry, and Jessie." He tapped each one on the shoulder as he said their names. "Children, this is Mr. Greene."

"Please," Max said with a soft chuckle, "call me Max. And," he added in a gentle voice, "I'm delighted to have such fine dinner companions."

Violet liked Max. He seemed a little shy, just like herself.

"Happy to meet you, Max," Benny piped up, shaking his hand. He thought Max looked handsome in his white pants and shirt, but what he liked best about him were his bright blue eyes.

Suddenly, three whistles blew, signaling it was time for the fire drill. Grandfather and the children hurried to their cabins, and from the closet shelves pulled down bright orange life jackets. Then they all reported to A Deck.

When the passengers were lined up, they were divided into small groups, and a sailor instructed each group on how to put on their bulky life jackets.

Henry helped Benny tie the cord. Jessie laughed. "You look like a small orange pumpkin, Benny," she teased.

Benny grinned. "And you look like a *big* orange pumpkin, Jessie."

The sailor blew a whistle for quiet. He motioned with his hand, and a lifeboat was lowered mechanically. It seated seventy-five passengers, but there were many other lifeboats for all the eight hundred passengers. In a real emergency, everyone would get into a boat and row away.

After the drill the children returned to their cabins and slipped into their swimsuits.

The children didn't see Max until dinnertime, for after lunch they spent the day at the swimming pool and then each chose a book from the library.

Grandfather had decided on the early sitting for dinner. Passengers could eat dinner at either 6:45 or 8:30.

The huge dining room gleamed with white linen, crystal chandeliers, fine china, and candlelight. The Aldens were led to table number thirty-eight.

Max stood up when he saw them. "Hello," he said. "Did you have a pleasant day?"

"You bet!" Benny said. "We swam and ate hamburgers by the pool. This afternoon we went to the library and got some books." He stopped to catch his breath. "What did you do?"

Max's thick eyebrows lifted, and he smiled. "Well, I strolled about the deck, played some shuffleboard on the forward deck, and talked to an elderly gentleman about World War Two. You see, I'm a history professor at Newton College."

All at once a waiter appeared, handing each a menu. "I'm your waiter, Ramos," he said.

"Hi, Ramos," Benny said. The menu was so big it slipped from his fingers. Ramos was quick to retrieve it.

"Shall I order for you?" Grandfather

asked, a twinkle in his eyes. The menu listed many appetizers, entrées, salads, and desserts. It was hard to know just what to order.

But soon decisions were made, and when Ramos brought the dinners they looked and smelled delicious.

All the Aldens had ordered the same meal. They had cold cucumber soup, thick roast beef, buttered potatoes, peas, and a tossed salad.

Max wanted the same meal, but he also ordered horseradish sauce. "Roast beef with horseradish sauce always reminds me of my great-aunt Edith," he said. "She loves horseradish and used to grow it in her garden. It was so strong I could hardly stand to take a bite."

"Can I try yours?" Benny asked. "I've never eaten horseradish sauce."

"Sure," Max said. "But just take a little bit."

Benny swallowed a small spoonful. His eyes grew big and he grabbed a glass of water.

"Wow!" he said. "That's the hottest stuff I ever ate!"

Everyone laughed.

"Do horses eat horseradish?" Benny wanted to know.

"Hmmm," Max said. "That's a good question."

Just then Ramos brought chocolate sundaes for dessert. When he had given everyone a sundae, he pulled an envelope out of his pocket and gave it to Max.

Henry saw that it was a telegram.

After reading it, Max's face paled, and he pushed his dinner aside. He excused himself and left.

What could have upset Max so much that he couldn't eat his dessert? Jessie wondered. They were having such a good time until the telegram came. What was wrong?

CHAPTER 2

The Tour

On Monday morning Violet awakened early. She hadn't slept well. It was her first night ever on a ship and she kept thinking of the deep water below her. What hid in those dark waters? Sharks? Old shipwrecks?

Jessie, sitting at the dressing table, brushed her long brown hair. She wore a white T-shirt and red shorts. She put down her brush and half turned. "Good morning, Violet. Are you finally getting up?"

Violet nodded. "I didn't sleep too well."

Quickly she jumped out of bed. "But I feel okay now." From the chest of drawers she took out a pair of jeans and a top. "I'll only be a jiffy in the shower."

Jessie waved a piece of paper. "Here's a list of today's activities. It was under the door when I got up. At ten o'clock there's a tour of the ship."

"That sounds like fun," Violet said.

It wasn't long before the girls joined Henry and Benny for breakfast. Grandfather had eaten earlier and was skipping the tour to play chess with Max.

The children went through the cafeteria line. Benny's eyes grew big at the mountain of fruit, the mounds of fresh pastry, cereals, eggs, bacon, sausage, waffles, pancakes, and fruit juices.

Benny's plate was piled high, but he ate every single bite.

After breakfast they hurried to join the tour. They went from deck to deck with the group.

"This is the kitchen," the tour guide said, moving into a huge room.

Henry gazed about the gigantic room. Lining the walls on one side were huge refrigerators with glass doors so you could see the food inside. On the other side of the kitchen were row after row of stoves.

Benny stood before a refrigerator staring at the luscious desserts.

"Would you like a taste?" a voice behind him asked.

Benny jumped but immediately answered, "Yes!"

A short plump man chuckled and came forward to open a refrigerator door. He pulled out a strawberry tart and handed it to Benny.

"Thanks!" Benny said, taking a bite.

"I'm Isaac," the chef said, adjusting his tall white hat.

"I'm Benny Alden, and over there are my brother and two sisters. This is certainly a *big* kitchen. I think I'd like to be a cook. I like to eat!"

"Well, Benny," Isaac said, smiling, "you can come to the kitchen again." He put his finger to his lips. "This is our secret.

Every time you come I'll give you a treat."

"Oh, I wouldn't take it unless I could help you," Benny said.

Isaac winked. "You would be a grand helper, I'm sure. And so would your brother and sisters." Isaac's white apron almost touched the floor as he reached for a bowl of blueberries.

"I'll be back," Benny promised.

"This way," the guide said.

They climbed the stairs to the navigation deck, which jutted above the sun deck. It was glass on all sides. The officer set Benny on a high stool where he could see for miles. Jessie studied the complicated instrument panel and the elaborate compass. Then they visited the engine room and radio room. After the tour they returned to B deck to play shuffleboard.

Grandfather, seated in a deck chair, put down his book. "Hello, children. How was the tour?"

Surprised, Violet turned around. "Fine, Grandfather," she said. "But I thought you and Max were playing chess."

"We were." Grandfather's face grew grave. "But Max suddenly said he didn't feel well and he left." He shook his head. "I'm afraid something is wrong, but Max won't talk about it."

Benny took the shuffleboard stick that Jessie handed him. "Why don't we just ask him?" he questioned, shoving the disk toward number ten, but it fell short of its goal.

Grandfather smiled. "Maybe he'll tell us when he's ready, Benny. We don't want to pry."

Benny thought this over. "No, I wouldn't want to do that."

After Henry won the game, the children ate lunch, then went out on deck. As they were leaning over the railing looking at the blue, shimmering sea, they heard someone on the ship-to-shore telephone.

"That's the radio room," Henry said, pointing at an open porthole.

"That's Max's voice," Violet whispered. The children couldn't help overhearing his words.

"Well," Max said, "I will, but only because you think I should. Yes, I'll do everything you told me." A few more words and he hung up.

Henry put his hands on his hips. "What do you make of that?"

Puzzled, Jessie wrinkled her forehead. "It sounds like he's doing something he really doesn't want to do."

"Who would make him do something he doesn't want to?" Violet questioned.

Henry looked at Violet and shook his head.

CHAPTER 3

New Passengers

On Tuesday, the third day of the cruise, Jessie and Violet were awakened by Grandfather. "We're sailing into St. Thomas," he called. "Come and see. Benny and Henry are already on deck."

It wasn't long before the five Aldens, hands resting on the rail, viewed the harbor scene. Cliffs on both sides of the port dropped into the sea. Many cruise ships, yachts, and sailboats were afloat on the turquoise water.

"St. Thomas is one of the Virgin Islands,"

Henry said. "I read about it in our guide book."

"It will be fun to look in the shops," Violet said. "We have six hours in Charlotte Amalie."

Confused, Benny said, "I thought this was St. Thomas."

"It is," Henry said with a chuckle. "Charlotte Amalie is the *capital* of St. Thomas."

"Oh," Benny replied. "*I* wish I could buy something in those shops."

"You can," Grandfather answered. "I want each of you to buy a good watch." He glanced at his grandchildren, delighted at their surprised faces. "On St. Thomas you'll find some of the best jewelry shops in the world."

"Grandfather!" Violet exclaimed, her face lighting with pleasure. "You're so good to us."

"I've been wanting a better watch," Henry said, with a broad smile. "My old one is always too fast or too slow."

"I'd *love* a new watch," Jessie said.

"I've never had a watch," Benny said, "except, of course, for Watch, our dog." The other Aldens chuckled. "But," he hastened to assure Grandfather, "I can tell time."

"I know you can, Benny," Grandfather said, placing his hand over Benny's.

All at once Benny shouted, "Look! A big fish jumped out of the water."

"It's a dolphin!" Violet said eagerly, watching it splash in the water.

A long black cruise ship sailed past, blocking their view.

Henry whistled. "That ship is twice as long as ours."

"It's called the *Viking*," Jessie said, reading the red letters on the prow. "It's a Norwegian ship. See the red flag with two blue stripes edged in white?"

Soon the *West Wind* was docked alongside the *Viking*.

After a hearty breakfast the children and Grandfather descended the ramp onto the streets of Charlotte Amalie.

The main street was lined with shops, but Grandfather led them to a store called The Watchman. There, the children tried on various watches until each one had chosen just the right one.

Proudly wearing their watches, the Aldens walked with Grandfather, peering in windows and exploring alleyways.

"All these shops were once pirate warehouses," Henry explained. "Blackbeard the pirate and Sir Francis Drake once walked these streets."

"Oh, Henry," Jessie teased. "Just because you read the guidebook you think you're an expert."

"I am." Henry laughed.

They stopped to rest at Emancipation Park, a small waterfront park. Next they went through Government House, where the governor lived, then they had lunch at an outdoor café.

"I'm ready to go back," Benny said, drinking the last of his milk.

Violet agreed.

"Then let's head for the ship," Grandfather said. "Is everyone ready?"

"Yes," Henry and Jessie echoed together.

Once on board the ship, Grandfather went

directly to his cabin, but the children lingered to watch a few new passengers check in with the first officer.

The arrivals were a burly blond man in a bright flowered shirt, a young girl in the ship's uniform, and a young couple with a crying baby.

"Hi, kids," the man in the tropical shirt boomed. "Do you like this cruise?" He reached over and grabbed Violet's hand, shaking it.

"It's been fine," she answered softly, astonished at how friendly this stranger was.

"My name's Tom Bishop," he stated, still pumping Violet's hand. "What's your name?"

"V-Violet Alden," she stammered, her face turning as pink as her T-shirt.

"I'm her brother, Henry," Henry said, stepping forward, "and this is Jessie, and — "

"And I'm Benny," Benny declared. "You've got big arms, Tom."

Tom threw back his head and laughed. He

flexed his arm, causing his muscles to bulge. "Soon as I'm unpacked, I'm heading for the exercise room." His small eyes squinted at Benny. "I could build you up to be a big boy, Benny."

"I *am* a big boy," Benny retorted, keeping his eyes fastened on Tom.

"Sure you are!" Tom paused. "I'll bet you kids know every inch of this ship."

"Of course we do," Benny said. "The exercise room is on C Deck."

"Thanks," Tom said breezily. "See you." He called over his shoulder, "I'll depend on you to show me around." He chuckled and climbed the stairs.

"He seems very friendly," Jessie said to the young woman who had finished signing aboard.

"Yes, he is," she answered. "He talks quite a bit."

Jessie laughed. She studied the girl, who wore a neat white skirt and jacket. "We're the Aldens."

"I-I'm Heather Kowalski, a new crew member," she said.

"Hi, Heather," Benny said. "We're pleased to meet you."

"Th-thanks." She looked embarrassed.

"Heather?" a steward asked, coming up to the young girl.

"Yes," she answered, turning.

He grinned, handing her a bunch of red roses. "These are for you." Then he added, "I couldn't help seeing the message. The flowers are from 'C' and he wishes you 'Good Luck.' " The steward gazed at Heather, who was very pretty. "I'm jealous. Who's C?"

"I must go." Hurriedly Heather backed away, then wheeled about and fled up the stairs.

Henry rubbed his chin. "She certainly was in a hurry to get away."

Jessie nodded. A baby's cry had startled her.

The mother looked apologetic as she shifted her tote bag to her hip and jiggled the baby up and down. "Shhh," she cooed softly. "It's all right, Robin. Shhh."

Violet removed her charm bracelet and

dangled it before the baby. The baby's eyes widened, and he stopped crying.

"Let me hold this for you," Henry offered, taking the mother's tote bag.

"Thanks," the woman said, handing the bag to Henry. "We're the Rands. I'm Melissa. This is Robin, who's nine months old, and over there, signing in, is my husband, Ralph. We've spent a week on St. Thomas, but we're ready to return to our home in Miami."

"I appreciate your help," Melissa said gratefully as a steward took their bags and the Rands started up the stairs.

"Melissa, I'll bet you this ship won't be nearly as good as ours," Ralph said.

Melissa laughed. "I wouldn't take that bet! Our ship was so wonderful!" With these words they disappeared into their cabin.

Jessie wondered what ship they could have been talking about. Nothing could be finer than the *West Wind*.

That night at dinner Melissa, Ralph, and Tom Bishop were seated at a table near the Aldens.

Tom bounced out of his chair and dashed over to their table. "Hi, kids. I had a great workout. Come to the exercise room tomorrow and I'll show you how I lift weights."

"You can lift weights?" Benny said, with enthusiasm. "Like in the movies?"

"Like in the movies," Tom repeated.

"Tom Bishop, this is our grandfather, James Alden," Henry introduced, "and our friend, Max Greene."

Tom reached over and heartily shook Grandfather's hand, then Max's. Max barely mumbled hello.

"See you tomorrow," Tom said, swaggering back to his table.

Max looked uncomfortable. "Excuse me," he said, rising. "I need to send a message. I'll be right back."

Violet spread her napkin across her lap, and glanced at Max's retreating back. "Why is Max so nervous?"

"I wish we knew," Henry answered.

Before they had finished their tomato soup, Max was back, his face pale. His hands were trembling as he picked up a spoon.

"What's wrong?" Jessie asked with concern.

"It's the radio room," Max answered. "No messages can be sent and none received. They're working on the problem, but in the meantime I need to send a message."

Henry wondered what had gone wrong with the radio. Poor Max, he thought. He seemed desperate to get in touch with someone.

CHAPTER 4

Trouble Aboard

After dinner the children went shopping. The ship's stores were well-stocked. Each child bought something. Violet bought a blue T-shirt with *West Wind* printed across a white cruise ship, Jessie a roll of film, Henry a pair of socks, and Benny a red T-shirt like Violet's.

They sauntered from one shop to another, halting at a jeweler's window to study the rubies, diamonds, and emeralds. Going on they looked in a toy store, which was filled with stuffed animals. Their final stop was at a ship's store with miniature cruise ships, sailor caps, and flags from all nations.

Grandfather had promised they could stay up for the late night buffet, so after shopping they walked around the deck, admiring the moonlit waters and the far-off lights of another cruise ship.

"Let's go by the radio room," Henry urged, "and see if they've fixed the radio."

"Good idea," Violet said. "I hope for Max's sake that it's repaired."

When they arrived at the radio room, several officers were talking.

"Hi," Benny said. "Can you send a message now?"

"Yes," replied an officer. His uniform, decorated with gold braid, was sparkling white. He smiled. "Did you wish to send one?"

"Not me," Benny hastily replied.

"We have a friend, though, who would like to," Jessie said.

"Do you mean Max Greene?"

"Yes," Jessie said, surprised that he knew

who she was talking about.

"The radio has been repaired, but Max Greene was in some time ago and used the phone," the officer said.

"Oh, good." Violet sighed with relief. She was pleased that Max had got his message through after all.

"What was the problem?" Henry questioned.

"Several wires had been pulled loose," the officer answered. "It wasn't difficult to repair."

Satisfied, Henry turned to the others. "Let's head for the late night buffet."

The officer chuckled. "Don't eat too much."

When they arrived at the grand ballroom, the display of food was spectacular. A dolphin ice sculpture dominated the colorful table of sandwiches, ham, cheeses, chocolate cakes, pies, ice creams, puddings, and coffee.

"What would you like?" Isaac asked, coming up behind Benny.

"Isaac!" Benny exclaimed, whirling about.

"I'm glad to see you. I'd like a taste of everything."

Isaac threw back his head and laughed. "Here," he said, pointing at a huge cake, "try this lemon cake. It's as light as a fleecy cloud."

"I'll have two pieces," Benny answered promptly.

Jessie smiled. "Save room for that luscious-looking strawberry pie, Benny." She turned to Isaac. "I'm Jessie Alden, this is Violet, and behind me is Henry. We saw you in the kitchen yesterday, but we didn't introduce ourselves."

Isaac bowed. "My pleasure!" He bustled to the counter and scooped up a cherry tart. "This is delicious," he said proudly, eager to please them. "It's one of my special-ties."

"Thanks," Violet said. "It's nice to have a chef tell us the best things to eat." She hesitated, then added shyly, "Benny said you might let us help out a little in the kitchen."

"That would be fun," Henry said, helping

himself to a large piece of coconut cream pie.

"How about tomorrow?" Isaac asked. "I need eight hundred dollops of whipped cream to top my raspberry tarts."

Benny's mouth formed a big O. "Eight hundred scoops of whipped cream. Wow! I'll be at the kitchen early."

"We all will," Jessie promised.

"Good," Isaac replied. "Come by anytime after ten o'clock."

"We'll be there," Henry said quickly, with a nod.

Frowning, Tom Bishop rushed by them. "Hello," he called briefly and then hurried on.

"Looks like Tom has other things on his mind than chatting with us," Violet said, sounding puzzled.

"Odd isn't it?" Jessie asked. "He's usually so friendly."

"Weird," Benny mumbled. "And just when I wanted to ask him how much weight he could lift!"

When they finished eating, they went back

on deck. They slowly stopped when they saw Heather. "Let's say hello," Violet said.

They waited patiently in the doorway until Heather had finished dictating a message to the radio man.

Heather tilted her head. "Just say, 'Thanks for the roses. Everything is going along fine.' End of message."

Jessie glanced at Henry, who lightly shrugged.

"Hi, Heather," Violet said.

"Oh," Heather said, looking up, "how are you?" She brushed by them as she hurried out. "I must go," she said apologetically.

"Let's find Max," Henry said, annoyed by Heather's coolness.

They went to the cafeteria where Max was sitting alone, drinking coffee. He called to them. "Hi, won't you join me?"

Henry sat next to Max. "The radio is repaired, Max."

"It doesn't matter," Max answered. "I phoned in my message." He still appeared agitated. "From now on, I'll use the phone. It's faster."

Max's business must be urgent, Violet thought.

"Do you want some dessert?" Benny asked, concerned that Max wasn't eating anything.

Max shook his head and a flicker of a smile crossed his face. "Thanks, Benny, but I've lost my taste for sweets."

Benny shook his head, not understanding how anyone could not like chocolate cake.

"As a matter of fact," Max said, "I'm waiting for the radio man to bring me an answer to the phone message that I left on my doctor's answering machine. I told the radio man where I'd be, so he should be here any minute."

"I'm glad," Jessie said. Maybe if his message was good news, Max could settle down and enjoy the voyage.

As they were talking, the radio officer approached Max. He leaned over and said, "I'm sorry, Mr. Greene, but no messages are coming through. It seems both the radio and the phone are out of order."

Nervously, Max jumped up, upsetting his coffee.

Quickly, Violet grabbed a handful of napkins and sopped up the hot liquid. She wondered what was going on. Surely this was no simple mechanical difficulty. Not when both the radio and the phone had been knocked out. Was someone deliberately causing trouble for Max?

CHAPTER 5

More Trouble

The first thing the children did the next morning was eat their breakfast and then hurry to the exercise room.

Tom, his sturdy legs pumping, sat astride a stationary bicycle. He wore a sweat band, but perspiration still poured down his face. "Good morning," he panted. "Be right with you."

Finally Tom stopped. Using the towel around his neck, he wiped his face. "Benny!" he said in a loud voice, "did you come to see me lift weights?"

"Yes!" Benny exclaimed. "How many pounds can you lift?"

"You'll see," Tom bragged, lying on a mat. With ease he lifted an iron bar with several twenty-pound iron disks.

"Wow!" Benny said, sounding amazed. "That's good."

"Just wait," Tom said with a cocky grin. He stopped and slid on heavier weights. Now he strained every muscle to raise the bar. Grunting with effort, Tom lifted the bar, then carefully put it down. Sitting up, he said between gasps, "Not bad, huh?"

"Super!" Benny said in an admiring tone.

"You certainly are strong, Tom," Violet said.

Tom rose to his feet. "Want to jog around the deck with me?"

Henry smiled. "I like to run, but we promised Isaac we'd help him out in the kitchen."

"Isaac?" Tom's blond eyebrows shot way up.

"He's a chef," Jessie explained.

"Oh," Tom said, uninterested. Then he gazed at Jessie. "You kids are pretty well acquainted around here, aren't you?"

"We know a few people," Violet admitted, staring at the floor.

"Do you know the boys in the radio room?" Tom questioned. "I hear they're having some trouble."

"Lots of trouble," Benny said firmly. "Our friend expected a message and it never came! That's 'cause nothing's working!"

"Well, well," Tom said, going over to chin himself on a nearby bar.

"We're going to figure out who did it," Benny said.

Tom, feet off the ground, stared at Benny. "Did what?"

"We think maybe someone tampered with the radio," Jessie explained patiently.

Tom went to the door. "Be careful," he advised, and jogged out.

Ralph Rand, in running shorts, came in. "Hi, everybody." He headed for the rowing machine. "It's a good time for a workout while Melissa is having her hair done," he said, giving them a wide smile.

"Where's Robin?" Jessie asked with concern.

"Don't worry." Ralph laughed. "He's in good hands in the nursery."

"Oh," Jessie said with relief. "Doesn't this ship have everything?"

Ralph shrugged. "It's not that great. Melissa and I used to work for a French cruise line and we had all the luxuries the *West Wind* has, and more." He turned and settled into the rowing machine, picking up the oars.

For a few minutes the children watched him as he strained at the oars, going faster.

At last, Jessie turned to Violet. "Don't you think we should leave?"

"Yes, I'm sure Isaac is waiting for us," Violet answered. "It's after ten."

When they arrived at the kitchen, Isaac had lined up hundreds of tarts. When he saw them, his eyes lit up. "I was hoping you'd come. He handed each of them a large bowl of whipped cream. "About this much," he said, spooning out a big tablespoonful.

"This will be fun," Benny said, heaping whipped cream on a tart.

"Not too much," Isaac cautioned.

For several hours the Aldens worked, helping Isaac finish the desserts. It was interesting to see bushel baskets of carrots, mountains of potatoes, and big roasts baking in the ovens.

"I've never seen so much food!" Benny exclaimed loudly. "Not even at the grocery store!"

Isaac chuckled. "It takes tons of food to feed eight hundred people." He filled a bag with five chocolate cookies. "Eat these later," he said with a wink. "And there's an extra one for your grandfather."

"Thanks, Isaac," Jessie said. "We'll be back."

The children said their good-byes and took the cookies back to their rooms, stopping to give one to Grandfather, who was reading on deck.

"We haven't explored the theater," Henry said. "Let's go to the upper deck."

They climbed the stairs and went into the empty theater. The red velvet seats, red carpet and walls, gave it a plush appearance.

When they came out, Heather rushed toward them. "I heard a splash on the deck below me! And someone yelled, 'Man overboard!' "

Henry ran to meet her, followed by Jessie, Violet, and Benny. Henry could tell by her face that she thought something awful had happened. "What do you think it is?" Then he dashed to the rail looking overboard. "Do you think someone fell in?"

"Yes! Yes!" Heather said, frantically nodding. "Or someone jumped in!"

"Over there!" Benny yelled, in an anxious voice. His eyes were wide as he stared at a round shape. "I see something!"

Jessie shaded her eyes. "It's only a dolphin, Benny. But you've got very sharp eyes."

"Man overboard!" Tom Bishop bellowed,

rushing past them. "Call the deck officer!"

But he needn't have yelled so loud, for sailors and the captain were already searching the sea. The ship sounded three alarms and began to circle the spot where Heather had heard the splash. The captain peered through a telescope.

"Who could have fallen in?" Violet asked in dismay.

"I don't know," Jessie replied, "but every minute is precious!"

Benny lifted off a life preserver. "I'll throw this in!" he shouted, staggering under its weight. "Whoever fell in can grab this and be saved."

"Good thinking, Benny," Henry said, but he reached for the life preserver and put it back. "Look, they've lowered a lifeboat and the sailors are rowing around the ship. Don't worry, they'll rescue anyone that's in the sea."

Passengers, gathering at the rail, scanned the waves for a glimpse of a swimmer or, worse, a body.

For an hour the search continued, then the captain strode by them. "Prepare the passengers for a head count," he ordered his lieutenant.

"Aye, aye, sir!" The lieutenant saluted smartly and ran to carry out the captain's orders.

Soon over the loudspeaker a voice commanded everyone to assemble at their lifeboat stations. "No life jackets are needed," the voice continued. "In ten minutes an attendance check will be made."

The children hurried to obey. As they dashed to their places, Jessie noticed something strange. Tom Bishop was squeezing himself into a small closet. "Tom!" she said forcefully. "You must go to your station. Now!"

"I thought I saw something in the water," he said, "and I just wanted to get a life jacket."

Jessie glanced in the closet where life jackets were stacked high. "No, Tom, hurry. Come with us! No one has been spotted overboard. It's time for the head count."

Reluctantly, Tom turned away and went to his station.

Quickly, sailors took the roll call. It wasn't long before the voice on the loudspeaker announced the happy news, "False alarm, ladies and gentlemen. We've been delayed, but now we're back on course. Please resume all normal activities."

"*Another* problem!" Max said anxiously. "What more can happen?"

Henry said in a puzzled tone, "What do you suppose the splash was that Heather heard?"

"I don't know," Violet said, "but it was odd, wasn't it?" She smiled. "I'm glad, though, that the captain keeps such close track of all his passengers."

"Whew," Benny said with relief. "I'm glad we don't have to worry about a drowned person anymore!"

"Me, too," Jessie said.

"Looking at all that water made me think of the pool," Benny said, wiping his forehead. "Let's go for a swim."

"Yes, let's," Jessie agreed, smiling. "I'm

glad everything turned out all right."

Violet grabbed Benny's hand. "Let's get our suits on."

At the pool the Aldens sat in the sun. Jessie, dangling her feet in the water, said thoughtfully, "Do you think someone delayed the ship on purpose?"

"Maybe," Henry said, shaking his head. "Look at all the strange things that have happened. First the radio goes out, then the phones, and now a mysterious alarm about a man overboard."

"What next?" Jessie said, frowning as she rubbed suntan lotion on her arms.

"Funny," Violet said, "but the phones and the alarm all happened after the new passengers came aboard."

"Max is acting pretty weird, too," Jessie said. "Maybe *he's* trying to sabotage the ship."

"It's scary," Benny said with a shiver. "But I don't want to think about it anymore. I'm going in the water."

Henry grinned. "Good idea, Benny." At the deep end he dived in and swam to the shallow water. "Come on in, Benny," he urged, holding out his arms.

Laughing with glee, Benny leapt in, followed by Violet and Jessie.

When they'd finished their swim, they ate hamburgers at the poolside café, then decided to top off their lunch by stopping at the ice cream bar. Benny ordered a banana split, Jessie a hot fudge sundae, Violet a chocolate shake, and Henry a butterscotch sundae.

In the afternoon the children relaxed in deck chairs alongside Grandfather, reading their books. The day had turned cloudy, and the sea became rough, whitecaps billowing on the high waves.

"This is fun," Benny said. "I like it when we go up and down."

Max joined them, sitting beside Grandfather. "That was very strange . . . the cry of 'man overboard,' wasn't it?" he questioned in a worried tone. He glanced anxiously over his shoulder.

"Max," Henry said boldly, "is something troubling you?"

"Maybe we could help you," Violet said softly.

Max glanced from one Alden to another. "Yes," he said, looking down at his clasped hands, "I do have a problem. I hope, though, that what has happened isn't putting friends such as you in danger." He rose. "I-I can't talk about it now." Head down, he walked away.

"Why won't Max confide in us?" Jessie asked.

"I think he will when he's ready," Grandfather replied.

Violet closed her book. She cared about Max, but maybe, she thought, *he* had caused all this trouble. It was up to them to find out what was going on.

CHAPTER 6

Sightseeing in San Juan

Max's problems were soon forgotten when the children arrived in San Juan, the capital of Puerto Rico. It was late afternoon, but they had a number of hours before the ship left at midnight.

The Aldens hurried down the ramp onto the narrow cobblestoned streets of Old San Juan. El Morro, the sixteenth-century fort, loomed ahead. The Aldens climbed up to the fort, now a museum. After exploring its many rooms, Grandfather urged them to go outside and wait for him. "I want to study this treaty," he said, indicating a yellow parchment in a glass case.

"We'll be resting under the trees," Benny said.

"Good," Grandfather replied. "Then we'll have our dinner at the Cat's Paw in New San Juan."

Once outside, Henry leaned back against a tree, a slight frown on his face. "I wonder what Max meant when he said he hoped he hadn't put us in any danger."

"I wonder, too," Violet said. "It's all *very* strange."

Benny's eyes widened. "I hope we don't have a shipwreck."

"I don't think we need to worry about that," Henry said with a chuckle.

Jessie said, "I'm sure Max knows what's behind all this."

Violet shook her head. "I hate to think he could be causing these things." She hesitated, then added, "But he's always in the middle of any problem."

Henry nodded. "Remember when we overheard Max on the phone? He said, 'I will, but only because you think I should. Yes, I'll do everything you told me.' " Henry rubbed his forehead. "I don't like to admit it, but those words sound pretty suspicious to me."

"I still say it's one of the new passengers," Jessie said. "Maybe it's Tom. He's strong and quick, too. He could pull out wires before anyone caught sight of him."

"Not Tom," Benny protested. "He's a good weight lifter, and exercise is all he cares about."

Violet sighed. "It's all very confusing. And the Rands are new passengers, but they're such a sweet family."

"Yes," Jessie said. "But they used to work for another cruise line."

"Maybe they're trying to hurt the *West Wind*," Benny said. "So their ship could get more passengers than ours!"

Henry shrugged. "I doubt it. I think Heather could be the one. Like the Rands, she's sweet, too. You need to remember that she knows the ship and, being a crew member, she can go anywhere she wants, *and* she's the one who heard the splash."

"She's always nervous," Jessie added, "and she never wants to talk to us for very long."

"And she received a telegram from C," Violet said.

"Yes," Henry said. "She could be working for this C. Remember the message she sent saying that everything was going along fine?"

Soberly, Jessie nodded. She hated to think that Heather could be so sneaky and underhanded, but she certainly acted very mysterious.

"Here comes Grandfather!" Benny shouted, standing and waving.

"Well, well," Grandfather said, coming nearer. "Are you solving all the ship's troubles?"

"Not really," Violet said, smiling. She rose and gazed about at the city below. "Isn't San Juan beautiful?"

"Yes, I just wish we had more time here," Jessie added.

"We'll make the best of the time we have,"

Grandfather assured her. "Let's go to our café."

"Yes!" Benny said. "I'm hungry."

They all laughed at the familiar words as they wended their way down to the narrow street below. The busy sidewalks were filled with people and the small shops were busy.

The Cat's Paw, a tiny café tucked away in an alley, had a small marimba band and a singer who sang in Spanish.

When they had finished eating a dinner of broiled chicken, browned rice with fresh pineapple, and a creamy pudding with caramel sauce for dessert, they walked back to the ship.

They arrived an hour before sailing and sat on the deck, waiting for the boat to sail.

"This is fun," Benny said. "I don't get to stay up this late very often."

At midnight, as the ship glided away from the dock, the Aldens watched the harbor lights gradually disappear into the darkness.

* * *

On Thursday morning, Jessie picked up the morning's bulletin which had been slid under the door and quickly scanned it. All at once she stopped and stared at the paper.

"What is it?" Violet asked anxiously.

Quietly, Jessie handed her the paper. "Due to engine trouble the ship will be delayed by a day."

"*Another* problem!" Violet said, shaking her head.

Jessie said slowly, "I'm getting scarcd. Not that I'd mind staying an extra day on the cruise, but do you think someone has deliberately tampered with the engine?"

"Let's see what Grandfather says," Violet said, opening the door. "He'll be at breakfast."

"No, let's not worry him. He's enjoying the cruise so much," Jessie said.

The girls met Henry, Benny, and Grandfather at their favorite table. As usual Benny's plate was heaped with pancakes, bacon, muffins, and fruit.

Ralph Rand stopped at their table. "Good morning," he said, holding a sleepy Robin. "How are the Aldens?"

"We're fine," Jessie said, smiling at the baby.

"Where's Melissa?" Violet asked, glancing around.

"Over there," Ralph motioned with his head, "loading up food on our breakfast tray."

"The chefs give a person enough to eat, don't they?" Henry said.

"Oh, I suppose so," Ralph replied. "But the French ship that we worked on had more delicious food." He gave a low chuckle. "And now this ship has engine trouble!"

"Oh, I'm sure we won't be delayed very much over a day," Grandfather said reassuringly.

"I'd like an extra day," Benny said. He looked up at Ralph. "Were you a chef?" Benny inquired.

"I was a steward, and Melissa was the social director. In fact, that's where we met."

"What's a social director?" Benny said curiously.

"Oh, she does things like planning Scrabble tournaments and dance contests," Ralph explained, shifting Robin's weight.

Melissa came up behind her husband and blew her baby a kiss. She said happily, "Isn't it a beautiful day?"

"The best!" Benny answered.

Ralph said, "We'll see you later. Have fun." The small family moved to an empty table.

"I like the Rands," Benny said. "But they act like the ship they worked on had better food than ours."

"I don't think that's possible, do you?" Henry asked, taking a bite of his spinach omelette.

"This food is the best I've ever tasted," Violet agreed.

Max paused at their table, his face white. "Hello," he said, attempting a smile. "How is everyone? Did you see the bulletin? We'll be delayed a whole day!"

"Sit down, Max," Grandfather urged.

"Have some breakfast. It might calm your nerves."

Max sat down, folding and unfolding his hands. He gazed at each Alden. "You've been so kind to me." He smiled briefly. "Even when I've behaved rather strangely."

"What's wrong, Max?" Henry questioned gently.

Max's blue eyes grew dark. "I think I owe every one of you an explanation. Do you have time to listen to my story?"

"Oh, yes," Jessie said, leaning forward. "Please tell us."

And so Max began his story.

CHAPTER 7

Max's Story

Gratefully, Max smiled at the waiter who put a cup of coffee before him. He took a deep breath. "My doctor, who also is a close friend, advised me to relax, and recommended this cruise." Max stirred his coffee. "It's been far from relaxing. The first night I received a telegram from my great-aunt Edith's lawyer saying that she had died." He paused, taking a sip of coffee. "I was very fond of her, even though she was rather eccentric. I felt sad and wanted to tell someone, but I'm rather reserved." He gave them a small smile. "As you may have guessed."

"I'm sorry about your great-aunt, Max. Now I realize why you were so upset," Jessie said.

"Wait," Max said. "There's more."

Benny's eyes were wide. "What else?" he asked.

"Great-Aunt Edith had written in her will that I must be present at the reading in order to inherit her beautiful old house." He finished his coffee. "I've always loved that old brick house and someday had planned to open it to the public so that everyone could enjoy it. The rooms are filled with marvelous antiques and artwork. And in the vault she kept her jewelry. Outside, gardens spread over several acres."

"Will you also inherit her money?" Grandfather asked.

"Yes, a large amount," Max answered. "I'd planned to use it for good causes."

"I'm sorry you lost your great-aunt," Violet said. "But I'm happy you'll inherit such a wonderful place."

Max looked down, shaking his head. "I'm afraid I won't inherit anything. You see the will is going to be read in Miami one week from the day I received the telegram. If I don't appear for the reading, the money and house will go to Great-Aunt Edith's only other surviving relative."

"Who's that?" Benny asked, forgetting to eat.

"My cousin, Carla," Max said. "I hate to say anything against anyone, but I know Carla. She's a mean selfish person, and I'm sure one of the first things she'll do is tear down Edith's house and sell all her beautiful things." He pushed his cup aside, and his lips tightened. "I can't let that happen."

"No, you can't." Violet nodded in agreement.

"When I first received the telegram, informing me of my great-aunt's death, I wanted to fly back immediately," Max said.

"Why didn't you?" Benny questioned carefully.

"I wish I had," Max said, answering Benny. "But when I called my doctor she told me to stay on the cruise. She said it'd do me good and I'd be back in time for the reading of the will." He shook his head. "She didn't know that this ship was going to have one problem after another."

Henry nodded knowingly. So that was the conversation they'd overheard on the phone. He remembered when Max told his doctor, "I will, but only because you think I should."

"When everything started to go wrong on the ship," Max said, "I tried to put the idea out of my head that someone was intentionally slowing the ship down. But when there was a false alarm about a person falling overboard, I was certain that *someone* was trying to keep me from getting to Miami on time."

"You're not the only one who's thought that," Jessie agreed. "We just couldn't figure out *why*."

"Now we know," Violet added quietly.

"But we still don't know *who's* doing it," Max said, tugging on his beard. "Carla isn't aboard."

"Maybe she's in disguise," Benny said.

"Maybe she hired someone to do the work for her," Henry suggested, "while she's hurrying to Miami. Someone like Heather," he added.

"So how do we catch this person?" Violet asked.

"We'll have to keep our eyes and ears open," Jessie said.

"And as soon as we get to the next port, I'm flying directly to Miami," Max said firmly.

"We'll be coming into Nassau Saturday morning," Grandfather said. "You should be able to get a plane to fly to Miami in plenty of time."

"I just hope nothing else goes wrong," Max said worriedly, "or I won't even make it to Nassau."

"Don't worry," Benny said. "We'll make sure you get there!"

"You've all been a big help," Max said,

leaning back with a smile. "I feel better already."

But he'd no sooner said these words when the ship lurched.

"What was that!" Max exclaimed, leaping up.

"I'm sure it's nothing," Grandfather said in a calm tone.

Max dropped into his chair. "I suppose you're right, but I'm tired of worrying. Sometimes I wish I could jump overboard and swim ashore." He smiled wearily. "I sometimes think I could beat this ship to Nassau."

"How about a game of chess?" Grandfather asked, clearly trying to take Max's mind off his problems.

Max rose. "Thanks, James. Perhaps later. Right now I need to take a brisk walk around the deck."

The children left Grandfather at his cabin, and went for a swim. Later they lunched by the pool.

After enjoying the sun and water, Jessie said, "Why don't we go to the social room

and see what's going on? Maybe we'll get into a Monopoly tournament."

"That would be fun!" Benny said, gingerly touching his sunburned nose.

Arriving at the beautiful room overlooking the sea, Henry noticed that a few passengers were playing cards, others were involved in a Scrabble game, but no tournament had been planned. Heather stood by Grandfather and Max's chess game.

"I see you're back at it again," Jessie said with a smile.

Grandfather nodded, as he moved a piece onto another square.

"Hi, Heather," Henry said.

Startled, Heather crumpled up a piece of paper she'd been reading. Then, remembering her job, she asked, "Can I help you find a game?"

Henry looked at Benny. "What do you think?"

"I'm ready to play Monopoly," Benny said.

"Me, too," echoed Violet and Jessie.

So for an hour they were occupied with buying and selling property, but when Violet won, Benny stood, and stretched. "What can we do now?"

"How about a movie?" Jessie asked. "I noticed the sci-fi classic *Spaceships and Spacemen* is playing."

Violet told Grandfather where they were going, and then she joined Henry, Jessie, and Benny. As they left the social room, Jessie noticed Heather setting up a cribbage board for Melissa and Ralph. She was surprised to see Heather, usually so shy, sitting down and talking to the Rands as if they were friends.

How strange, Jessie thought. She shrugged and hurried to catch up with the others. It probably didn't mean anything, but they'd promised Max to keep their eyes open and she intended to report anything unusual.

They settled in center row seats in the movie theater and watched *Spaceships and Spacemen*. The exciting movie lasted more than two hours, and when they came out

Benny had a suggestion. "I'd like an ice cream cone."

"Dinner is going to be served soon," Violet said.

As they walked by the soda fountain they noticed Tom Bishop hunched over a drink.

"Well," he said, twirling about on the seat, "if it isn't the Aldens. Sit down and tell me the latest news."

Benny climbed up on a stool. "We don't have any news," he said.

Good for Benny, Henry thought. He was afraid Benny might say something about Max and the will, and that wasn't anyone's business.

"I noticed your grandfather was playing chess with Max — Max — what was his name?" Tom questioned.

"Max Greene," Jessie replied, slowly and cautiously.

"That's right," Tom said. "Max Greene." Through his straw, he slurped up the last of his diet cola. "It looks like we're going to be late getting into Miami." He chuckled, flexing his arm muscles. "That's okay by me. I could use a couple more days in the exercise room. Why does that Max Greene look so worried?"

"Don't know, Tom." Benny hopped down from his stool. "We've got to go or Grandfather will worry."

Tom waved. "Well, then I guess I'll see you children later."

The children went back to their cabins and dressed for dinner. Grandfather met them, and they all went up on deck to look at the beautiful sky.

At six-thirty, they headed for the grand dining room where Ramos served a dinner of roast pork with dressing, mashed potatoes, broccoli, and apple and celery salad. Chocolate cake was the dessert.

"I hate to leave the *West Wind* and you, Ramos," Benny said, looking sad. "And all this terrific food."

"I will miss you, too," Ramos answered. "But you still have two more dinners. And," he added proudly, "Saturday night is special."

"It's our farewell dinner, isn't it?" Jessie asked.

"Yes, and what a dinner!" Ramos said, rolling his eyes. "You will like it!"

After the children had eaten their strawberry pie, they strolled about the deck with Grandfather.

"On Saturday morning you'll see Nassau," Grandfather said. "You'll enjoy the Straw Market in the center of town."

"I'll enjoy seeing Max off first," Violet said. "I'm worried that he won't get back to Miami by Sunday. If he doesn't he'll lose everything."

"Don't be concerned, Violet," Grandfather said. "It's a short flight from Nassau to Miami."

Maybe so, Violet thought, but we still have Friday to get through, and she had a nagging fear that someone was plotting something else to keep Max from reaching his destination. She shivered slightly. It was scary when you didn't know what to expect.

CHAPTER 8

Slowdown

The next morning after breakfast, the children climbed the steps to A Deck where the Ping-Pong tables were located.

Benny teamed with Henry against Jessie and Violet. The small white ball flew back and forth. Although Henry hit the ball so hard that Jessie often missed it, the girls eventually won. The winners' reward was to choose the next activity.

"Let's see," Violet said, "what should we do next?"

Benny, fingers crossed, stared at her as if willing her to choose his favorite.

"Shall we go shopping?" Jessie asked.

Benny wrinkled his nose.

"Or should we go swimming?" Violet questioned.

Eagerly, Benny shook his head.

"Swimming and lunch by the pool would be nice," Jessie said. "It will be our last day to do this."

"We've got tomorrow," Benny said hopefully.

"Tomorrow is Saturday, and we sail into Nassau," Henry explained. "We'll be ashore most of the day."

"Oh," Benny said, nodding. "That's right. I forgot."

The Aldens hurried to the pool and spent the rest of the morning swimming, and eating hotdogs and drinking milkshakes for lunch.

Later, as they sat on deck reading their library books, Heather walked by. "Hello," she said, stopping briefly. "I see you're having a little quiet time."

"I don't feel quiet," Benny said, holding up his book. "I'm reading *The Missing Dog Mystery*."

"Is it exciting?" Heather asked.

"Very!" he exclaimed.

"Sit down, Heather," Jessie offered and she smiled, pointing to the empty chair next to her.

Heather shook her head, then glanced around and saw Melissa Rand. "I'm sorry. I can't," she said abruptly, and hurried to catch up with Melissa. The two walked down the deck and disappeared around the corner.

"Isn't that weird?" Violet said in a puzzled voice. "Heather never has time for us, yet she seems to have time for the Rands. I wonder why."

Jessie frowned. "I wonder, too. She's always hurrying away from us."

"It's as if Heather's afraid of us," Henry said. "Maybe," he speculated, "she's trying to hide something."

"Remember when she first came on board?" Violet asked.

"Yes," Jessie replied. "Heather received roses from 'C'!"

Henry nodded. "Could the 'C' stand for Carla?"

"Oh, no!" Violet said, horrified. "You mean Carla might be paying Heather to help her?"

"Yes," Jessie answered sadly. "That's why Heather doesn't want to talk to us!"

"I think Heather's just bashful," Benny said, then added with a grin, "like Violet."

Violet's cheeks grew slightly pink, but she smiled.

Henry closed his book. "The Rands used to work for a French cruise ship," he said thoughtfully.

"It's possible," Henry continued, rising, "that the Rands could have been hired by their French ship."

"And," Violet said, "they're trying to sabotage the *West Wind* because it's a rival cruise ship."

"That way, their ship would get more passengers," Jessie said. "But we have no *proof* of any of this!" Changing the subject because she was so puzzled, she asked, "Who wants to play shuffleboard?"

"I do," Henry replied.

"Me, too," Violet said.

Benny leaped up. "Me, three!" he echoed. "I'm ready to go."

So the four Aldens headed for the shuffleboard deck. Tom Bishop, standing by a Coke machine, received a telegram from the steward. Hastily, he read the words, then stuffed it in his jacket pocket when he saw the children. "Hi, kids," he called. "What's happening?"

"Not much, Tom," Benny said, taking a shuffleboard stick. "Want to play a game with us?"

"Why, not?" he asked, taking off his jacket and rolling up his sleeves. As he removed his jacket, the telegram gently fluttered to the deck.

The game didn't last long. Tom won, and he laughed. "Next time," he said, putting on his jacket, "we'll play Monopoly. I'll bet you

can beat me at that." With a wave, he was gone.

Jessie put up her shuffleboard stick, and as she did so she noticed Tom's telegram. She picked it up and read the words: JUST TWO MORE DAYS AND WE'LL BE RICH! CARLA.

"What do you suppose this means?" Jessie asked worriedly, handing the telegram to Henry.

After reading it, Henry frowned. "Two more days of what?"

Violet took the telegram. "How could two more days make them rich?"

Jessie was thoughtful. "If Max makes it to Miami on time, *he'll* be rich. If not his cousin Carla will inherit Great-Aunt Edith's estate. This telegram could be from cousin Carla."

Henry picked up Jessie's train of thought. "And Tom could have been hired by Carla to keep the *West Wind* from getting to Miami on time."

"Then Tom has been the one all along," Violet said, disbelief on her face.

"And he seemed so nice, too!" Benny exclaimed.

"Let's find Max," Henry said. "I'm sure he'll know what to do."

They found Max and Grandfather playing cards in the library.

"Here, Max," Jessie said, "I think you should read this."

Max stared at the telegram, then his eyes lit up in understanding. "Tom Bishop. Of course. He must be Thomas, the man Carla's going to marry. She talked about a 'Thomas.' I've never met him so I had no idea what he looked like."

"He did ask us questions," Henry said, "and once he mentioned how upset you looked."

"When Tom came aboard," Benny said, "I remember he said that we kids knew all about the ship, and we'd have to show him around."

"That's right," Violet said.

"So," Max said, "Tom's doing Carla's dirty work! Carla's probably in Miami right now!" He shook his head. "If I don't get to Miami by Sunday, she'll inherit everything!"

Henry said, "We need to warn the captain about Tom."

"Yes," Jessie agreed. "And let's also ask him if we'll be sailing into Nassau on time."

"Good idea," Grandfather said, rising to his feet.

They found the captain on the navigation deck, and when he heard their news, he was furious. "*No one* can tamper with my ship!"

Thoughtfully he added, "I'm not surprised, though. The crew has seen Tom outside the engine room a few times and wondered what he was up to."

"He's deliberately trying to delay the ship," Max said urgently. Then he explained to the captain why he had to get to Miami.

"Well," the captain said, "Tom Bishop won't succeed. We're right on time. We're taking a shorter route to Nassau." He smiled.

"So, Mr. Greene, you'll be at the reading of the will."

Max breathed a sigh of relief.

"We're on time now," Grandfather said, "but what if . . .?"

"What if Tom does something else to sabotage the ship?" Jessie finished.

"Exactly," Grandfather said.

For a few minutes they were all silent. Then Jessie, her eyes shining, said, "I have a plan."

"You have?" Violet asked.

"Yes, I have," Jessie replied, smiling. And she whispered into the captain's ear, and then into Max's.

The captain nodded. "I'll do it," he said firmly.

A slow grin spread across Max's face. "Good idea, Jessie," he said.

"What are they going to do?" Benny asked as they walked back to the cabin.

"You'll see at dinner," Jessie said with a secret smile.

The Aldens went to their cabins to change clothes, and met at their table for dinner.

Tom was sitting at the next table, right behind Max.

"I can't wait to see what the captain's
going to do," Benny whispered carefully to
Jessie.

"He's going to say something to Max,"
Jessie carefully whispered back. "Listen
closely."

As they ate their lemon meringue pie,
the captain walked slowly by the Aldens'
table.

"Excuse me, Captain," Max said quietly,
beckoning the captain to move closer. "It's
urgent that I know. Will we be in Nassau on
time?"

The captain looked grave. "Well, I didn't
want to alarm the whole ship, but we've had
another problem with the engine," the captain told Max in hushed tones. "We can't
travel at the usual speed. So we'll be delayed
another couple of days."

Benny glanced at Jessie and smiled. Now
he knew what she'd whispered to the Captain
and Max.

Henry smiled, too. Jessie had told the captain to fib a little — to tell Max there'd be a delay, when truthfully the ship was right on time. And to say it just loud enough for Tom to overhear.

Violet watched Tom. He was leaning closer to hear the captain's words. She saw a nasty grin light up his face. Tom glanced at Max to see how he took the news.

"Isn't there anything you can do?" Max asked.

"No, I'm afraid not," the captain said.

When Max excused himself abruptly and left the table, Tom almost laughed aloud. He didn't realize that Max was only *pretending* to be upset. Everything was going according to Jessie's plan. The captain had played his part perfectly.

Then why did she still have this uneasy feeling?

CHAPTER 9

The Guilty One Confesses

On Saturday morning the Aldens leaned over the rail as the *West Wind* sailed into Nassau, the capital of the Bahama Islands, and docked at Prince George wharf.

"It will take a while before we're able to go into town," Grandfather said. "They need to prepare the ramp for disembarking. Right now, let's have breakfast."

"I can't wait to see Nassau's Straw Market," Violet said.

"It's big," Grandfather said. "You'll have fun there."

The children went through the line, heaping their plates with their favorite food and fruit.

"The steward told me we'll be free to go ashore in one hour," Grandfather said.

"Good!" Benny said. "It's our last stop before we go home, and I want to see everything."

"And you will," Grandfather promised, chuckling.

While they were lingering over breakfast, Max rushed toward them. "The captain and I are going to confront Tom Bishop. Will you come along?"

"You bet!" Henry said, jumping to his feet.

Jessie hurried alongside Henry, her heart beating hard. What would Tom say? What would he do?

"Maybe he's in the exercise room," Benny said.

"Let's try his cabin first," the captain said. "Usually when we're about to go ashore passengers are getting ready in their rooms."

The captain rapped on Tom's door. No answer. He knocked louder.

Finally, Tom flung open the door and stared sleepy-eyed at the captain, Max, and the Aldens. "What do you want?" he asked in an annoyed tone. "You woke me up!"

"We need to talk to you. It's about what's been happening on my ship," the captain said sternly.

"What are you talking about?" Tom asked angrily, his face flushing a deep red. "I had nothing to do with the ship's delay or anything else!"

"Yes, you have!" Max said. "What about this?" And he thrust the telegram in Tom's face.

Tom grabbed the wire, and his face grew white.

"You're in this with Carla, aren't you, Thomas?" Max said, folding his arms across his chest and waiting for an answer.

"No, I'm not!" Tom sneered. "And you'd better watch who you're accusing or you'll end up with a lawsuit!"

Suddenly, Benny shouted, "What's this?"

And he dashed toward an iron box sticking out from under the bed. He pulled it out.

"It's a toolbox," Henry said, kneeling down and examining hammers, pliers, and screwdrivers.

"So what if I do own a toolbox." Tom snorted. "Is that a crime?" Behind his boldness, though, he appeared shaken.

Benny lay on the floor, peering under the bed. "I've found something else!" he yelled. "This!" He hauled out a rod-shaped piece of iron.

The captain swooped down on the piece, holding it up in triumph. "This is a part that was taken from the engine!" He glared at Tom. "Now what do you have to say for yourself?"

Tom stepped backward, bumping into the dresser.

"Admit it, Tom," Max said. "Do you want to take all the blame and let Carla off scot-free?"

"All right," he growled. "So I tried to slow down the ship. Will I be sent to prison for that?"

The captain looked solemn. "What you have done is very serious, Mr. Bishop. You also kept messages from being sent and from coming in!"

"And what about shouting 'Man overboard'?" Henry said sternly.

"I only wanted to delay the ship. I didn't mean any harm." He glared at them.

"And you tried to hide in a closet so you couldn't be counted," Jessie said, tightening her lips.

Tom bent his head. "Yes," he confessed. "I'm engaged to Carla." He shot Max a hateful look. "We wanted to stop you from getting everything." He paused, then snapped, "You always were Great-Aunt Edith's favorite!"

"I've called ahead, Mr. Bishop," the captain said calmly, "and the police are waiting for you in Nassau."

"Who cares!" He gave Max a wicked smile. "At least you'll be late coming into Miami! You won't get a penny!"

"Look out your porthole, Tom." Jessie said.

Tom glanced at her, then rushed to the porthole. His mouth dropped open. "We're in Nassau!" He exclaimed in confusion. Whirling about, he faced the captain. "You announced we'd be delayed a day!"

"Yes," the captain said, chuckling. "We played a trick on you." He nodded in Jessie's direction. "Give that young lady credit for a good idea!"

"We've lost," Tom muttered, sinking down on his bed.

"You'll be locked in your cabin until we go ashore," the captain said.

Tom didn't reply, still shaking his head in disbelief.

The captain and Max left, followed by the Aldens.

Sadly, Benny turned and gave Tom a last look. "I'm sorry, Tom. I liked you, but you did bad things."

Tom covered his face with his hands.

"Good-bye, Tom," Benny said softly, closing the door.

The captain locked Tom in, and they went up on deck.

"Thanks for your help," the captain said. "You children are good detectives." He moved toward the stairs. "Now I need to prepare for the passengers getting off at Nassau." With a wave he was gone.

So it's over, Violet thought. Instead of gaining money, Tom and Carla are going to end up in prison.

"Hurry up, Violet," Jessie urged. "Let's see Nassau!"

CHAPTER 10

The Straw Market

Once the all clear sounded, the Aldens and Max hurried down the ramp onto Bay Street.

Grandfather reached over and shook Max's hand. "Good luck!" he said.

"I'll make it," Max said. "Thanks for all your help!"

The chidlren waved good-bye, for Max was already rushing to a taxi.

"To the airport!" Max shouted and jumped into the cab.

"I'm glad Max is on his way," Jessie said,

breathing a sigh of relief.

"I'm glad, too," Grandfather said. "He'll soon be in Miami."

"Won't Carla be surprised to see him?" Violet said with a smile.

"There's the police," Henry said happily, pointing to two officers in white Bermuda shorts.

"They're waiting to arrest Tom," Jessie said.

"Could we hurry?" Benny asked. "I don't want to see Tom in handcuffs."

"Yes," Grandfather said. "We only have six hours to see everything. We want to be back in plenty of time for our special farewell dinner."

"Right!" Benny agreed.

They walked down a narrow street toward an open air market.

While the children wandered through the stalls of straw crafts, Grandfather drank coffee at a nearby café.

Benny stopped at the straw hats. Jessie, reaching for a tall hat with a big brim, said with a smile, "Here, try this one on, Benny."

She set it on his head, and it slid down to his nose. "It's too big," Benny complained good-naturedly.

Laughing, Violet said, "I agree!" She removed his hat and tried on a smaller one. "There!" She stepped back. "That fits fine."

"You look like a cowboy, pardner," Henry teased.

Benny grinned. "I feel like one, too." And he hooked his thumbs in his belt, made a comical face, and circled Jessie and Henry.

Still chuckling, Jessie tried on a red wide-brimmed hat. "I love this." She paid for both hats, and they moved on to visit some other shops.

Just as they had finished exploring and were about to leave to rejoin Grandfather, they met Heather. The young girl, dressed in a spotless white uniform, had a package under her arm.

"Hi!" Benny said. "What did you buy, Heather?"

A smiled crossed her face. "Just a doll for my niece."

"Would you like to walk back to the ship with us?" Violet offered.

"N-no," Heather answered immediately, backing away. "I'm not quite ready." With these words, she turned on her heels and disappeared among the piles of straw purses.

Puzzled, Henry stared after her, "She's *still* not very friendly," he mumbled. Then in a louder voice, he said, "Let's find Grandfather or he'll be worried."

As they arrived at the café, Grandfather pushed away his cup and looked about. When he glimpsed his granchildren, his eyes lit up. "Shall we return to the ship for dinner? We mustn't miss this one!" he said mischievously.

"Yes!" Benny answered emphatically. "I'm hungry."

Henry laughed. "So, what else is new?"

Climbing up the ramp, the Aldens went directly to their cabins and put away their new straw purchases. They showered and dressed in their nicest clothes for the big farewell dinner.

Grandfather and the four children went into the dining room together.

Ramos handed each one a menu, which listed item after item.

"I don't know what to choose," Violet said, looking at the long list of appetizers. "Shall I get a hot appetizer or a cold one?"

"You may have both," Ramos said, "but the stuffed mushrooms are especially good."

Violet gave him a grateful smile. "I'll have that."

"I can't decide between the cream of asparagus soup, the vichyssoise, or the oxtail soup," Henry said.

"What's Vee-shee-swozz?" Benny asked.

"Cold potato soup," Henry answered.

"I want that," Benny announced.

Each Alden decided on the Caesar salad, roast turkey, dressing, mashed potatoes, and gravy.

As they finished, all at once the room became dark. Trumpets blared, and in marched two lines of waiters, bearing trays of flaming dessert.

Ramos stopped at their table and set before

them baked Alaska, which was ice cream covered with meringue and drizzled with hot fudge, and topped with flaming cherries.

Benny's mouth formed a huge O. "I've never seen such a wonderful dessert!" he exclaimed.

Grandfather laughed. "I'm sure you won't want a sundae tonight!"

Benny patted his stomach. "No, sir!"

"There's bingo in the library," Jessie said, scooping up the last of her ice cream.

"Let's go," Henry said. "The magic show doesn't start until nine-thirty."

So they played a game of bingo, then went into the grand ballroom for the magic entertainment.

The opening act was a juggler who did all sorts of tricks with three golden tenpins. Next was a magician who pulled a rabbit out of a hat, and sawed a woman in two. For his final act the band struck up "Yankee Doodle Dandy," while from his sleeve the magician drew yards and yards of silk flags.

Benny's foot kept time to the lively music, and when it was over, he turned to Henry, saying, "I wish there was more."

Henry looked at his watch. "Do you know it's midnight?"

Benny gave Henry a sidelong glance. "Really? I could stay up this late every night."

"No way," Henry said. "It was a good show, though, wasn't it?"

"The best!" Benny said.

"Time to go to our cabins," Grandfather said.

That night Violet went to bed with a smile on her face. What a wonderful day. They had not only seen Nassau, but a magic show as well. It was hard to believe that tomorrow they'd return to Miami. She was sorry to see the end of the cruise, but it would be good to get home, too.

CHAPTER 11

Sailing Home

On Sunday, after the children had finished packing and eaten their breakfast, Benny said, "Let's visit my favorite place."

"And where's that?" asked Henry. "The navigation deck?"

"No," Benny replied, grinning.

"The pool?" Violet asked.

"Nooo."

"The dining room?" Jessie teased.

"Not the dining room, either," Benny said.

"Then, where?" Violet asked, sounding puzzled.

"I want to visit Isaac!" Benny loudly announced.

"Ah," Henry said with understanding. "The kitchen. I should have guessed that was it."

"Yes, Benny," Jessie said. "We must all say good-bye to Isaac. We dock in Miami at noon, so we have time to do some visiting, too."

"The ship feels like home, now," Violet said.

Henry laughed. "True. We know the ship from the engine room to the top of the navigation deck."

"Follow me!" Benny said, leading the way to the kitchen.

Isaac, cleaning a refrigerator door, stopped when he saw the children and a wide smile creased his face. "Come in, come in," he said, taking off his tall white hat and wiping his brow. "Did you come to say good-bye?"

"Yes," Benny said, feeling sad.

"I'm sorry to see you go, but you've all enjoyed yourselves, haven't you?" Isaac asked.

"Oh, yes," Violet said.

"I wish I had a treat for you, but everything has been wrapped and put away." Isaac put a finger to the side of his nose, thinking. "Wait. I think there's a package of chocolate chip cookies that I could give you," he said.

Jessie laughed. "We just finished eating breakfast, Isaac. Besides, we didn't come for any sweets. We came because you're our friend."

"No, no, I insist," Isaac said, snapping his fingers. "I know! I have something you'll like even better than chocolate chip cookies." He went to a freezer, taking out a plate holding four, giant chocolate-covered strawberries. He offered them to the children. "Taste these!"

Each Alden took a strawberry. Biting into his, Benny rolled his eyes. "Hmmmm, good."

Isaac laughed. "I thought you'd like

them." He set his hat squarely on his head and solemnly stuck out his hand, shaking hands forcefully with Henry, Violet, and Jessie. Finally, he turned to Benny and scooped him up in his arms. "You've been my helper, Benny, and I'm glad I met you."

"And I'm glad I met you," Benny said happily.

"We must go," Jessie said. "We have others we want to see."

"I'm sure you do," Isaac said. "You've made friends with many people on this cruise."

"Except for Tom Bishop," Henry said grimly. Then, with a wave and a smile, he added, "Good-bye, Isaac."

They left to find Heather, who was in B Salon helping passengers with any questions and making sure their luggage was tagged.

Grandfather was getting instructions for leaving the ship.

Heather was tying tags on a woman's luggage. Turning around, she smiled. "Hello,

Aldens! I'm glad you came by." She pointed to a comfortable sofa and matching chair. "Let's sit over there."

Jessie was surprised at how friendly she was. Usually Heather didn't care to talk at all.

Heather folded her hands in her lap. "I'm sure you've wondered why I always ran away when I saw you."

Henry just waited, not wanting to tell her how unfriendly he thought she had been.

Heather continued, "You know, this was my first job." She twisted her ring. "I'm quite shy, and meeting all these passengers made me even shyer."

"Is that why you didn't stay and talk to us?" Benny asked.

Heather's cheeks flushed pink, but she smiled. "Yes. It wasn't because I didn't want to stay and chat with you. I was grateful for how warm and friendly you were. In fact, now that I know the crew and have met people like you, I feel much more relaxed." She gave them a warm look. "Now I enjoy my work. Since I've finished work on my first cruise, I know the next one will be even easier."

Jessie reached over and touched Heather's hand. "Now we understand why you seemed a little distant. Tell me, who is C, the one who gave you the roses? Was it your boy-friend?"

Heather gave a light laugh. "My brother Charles. He wished me good luck, knowing how nervous I was on my first job. I sent him a message back, telling him that every-thing was going fine."

"You crumpled up a piece of paper when we came to play Monopoly," Benny said.

"Yes, it was another message from Charles. I knew I shouldn't have been read-ing it when I was working." She smiled imp-ishly. "Although I should've known that you wouldn't have minded."

Violet smiled. To think they had sus-pected this sweet girl just because she'd been so quiet and nervous.

All at once Heather reached into a bag

beside the sofa. "I have something for each of you."

Benny's eyes grew big as she pulled out four white caps with visors.

Heather first gave a cap to Benny, then to Henry, Violet, and Jessie.

"Great!" Benny said, pulling the billed cap down to his eyes and grinning.

The caps had the words "West Wind" around the band. "Thank you, Heather!" Jessie said, trying hers on. "I'll wear it home."

"I'll wear mine, too," Violet said, sounding delighted.

Henry wore his rakishly to one side. "Now everyone will know we're all from one family!"

"Oh, there are the Rands," Heather said, standing.

"Did you know them before the cruise?" Henry asked.

"No," Heather said. "But I've been helping Melissa with Robin, and we've become friends. That's why I felt relaxed with them and not at all nervous."

The Rands came closer. Ralph, holding Robin, smiled when he saw the Aldens. "I was hoping we'd find you before we left. I wanted to say good-bye."

"And so do I," Melissa said, shaking hands with each of them. "You've always been so friendly."

Ralph chuckled. "I'm afraid we've been comparing the *West Wind* to the French line we were on, but truthfully this ship is fantastic. We like everything about it. Especially passengers like you."

"You even bet your ship was better than the *West Wind*!" Benny said.

"Yes," Melissa said with a laugh. "But we learned otherwise." She took Ralph's hand. "We must go."

"Maybe we'll meet again," Melissa said, happily.

"I hope so," Henry answered.

The Rands moved on.

"I must go, too," Heather said, blowing them a kiss. Then she was gone.

Grandfather, who was filling out some papers, called to them. "Do you all want to go out on deck? We're just coming into Miami!"

"Yes," Jessie said. "We were so busy saying good-bye to everyone that we almost forgot to see our port."

The children went out on deck, and over the blue water loomed the white buildings along Miami's coast. Closer and closer they came.

A steward came by. "We'll be docking in fifteen minutes. Please wait until the all clear is given for disembarking."

The children went inside, found Grandfather, and sat with him.

Before long, over the loudspeaker, a voice said, "All passengers prepare to disembark."

The Aldens moved along with a large group and went out on deck.

Down the ramp they hurried.

"There're lots of people beyond the gate," Violet said.

"Yes, they've come to meet their friends," Grandfather said.

Suddenly, through the crowd, Jessie

glimpsed Max. "Look! It's Max!" she shouted.

Sure enough, when they went through the gate, Max rushed forward to meet them.

"Hello!" he called, catching up to them.

"Max!" Henry said. "We're glad to see you!"

"How did you come out with the will?" Jessie asked anxiously.

"I was in time. I inherited the house and the money." Max, who had always seemed so upset before, now appeared to be full of joy.

"Oh, I'm happy!" Benny said. "We were scared Carla might beat you."

"No, I made it with plenty of time to spare," Max said. "And when I open the house to the public, I want you to be my first guests. I'll give you a private showing!"

His smiled broadened. "If it hadn't been for you, I never would have gotten Great-Aunt Edith's house. Tom and Carla would have."

Grandfather pumped Max's hand. "Wonderful, Max. I wish we could stay and help you celebrate, but we have a plane we have to catch."

"I understand," Max said, smiling, "but I just wanted to share my good news with you!"

"Good-bye, Max," Jessie said, and smiled. "Maybe we'll see you again someday soon. Maybe we can come and visit you."

After they'd all wished Max good luck and good-bye, Benny said firmly, "I don't like good-byes. I don't like to say good-bye to people. It doesn't seem fair."

"Yes, but think of the new friends you made," Violet said. "Think of people like Issac and Max."

"Besides," Henry said, and he laughed. "We can always look forward to seeing them again."

Benny's face brightened. "That's right. Maybe we'll see Max and Isaac next year."

"Hurry, children," Grandfather exclaimed. "We need to catch a taxi to the airport."

Once in the cab, Jessie glanced over her shoulder to look at the *West Wind* for the last time. It had been a wonderful trip, but now they were going home. That would be wonderful, too.

GERTRUDE CHANDLER WARNER discovered when she was teaching that many readers who like an exciting story could find no books that were both easy and fun to read. She decided to try to meet this need, and her first book, *The Boxcar Children*, quickly proved she had succeeded.

Miss Warner drew on her own experiences to write each mystery. As a child she spent hours watching trains go by on the tracks opposite her family home. She often dreamed about what it would be like to set up housekeeping in a caboose or freight car — the situation the Alden children find themselves in.

When Miss Warner received requests for more adventures involving Henry, Jessie, Violet, and Benny Alden, she began additional stories. In each, she chose a special setting and introduced unusual or eccentric characters who liked the unpredictable.

While the mystery element is central to each of Miss Warner's books, she never thought of them as strictly juvenile mysteries. She liked to stress the Aldens' independence and resourcefulness and their solid New England devotion to using up and making do. The Aldens go about most of their adventures with as little adult supervision as possible — something else that delights young readers.

Miss Warner lived in Putnam, Connecticut, until her death in 1979. During her lifetime, she received hundreds of letters from girls and boys telling her how much they liked her books.